WITHDRAWN

MICHAEL DAHL PRESENTS

PHOBIA

No Escape

A TALE OF TERROR BY BRANDON TERRELL
ILLUSTRATED BY MARIANO EPELBAUM

STONE ARCH BOOKS
a capstone imprint

Michael Dahl Presents is published by Stone Arch Books,
A Capstone Imprint
1710 Roe Crest Drive
North Mankato, Minnesota 56003
www.mycapstone.com

Library of Congress Cataloging-in-Publication Data is available on
the Library of Congress website.

Summary: Jake Prescott thinks he's finally in luck when magician
Augustus Towers asks him to be his assistant. Jake's an amateur
magician, and Augustus might be the perfect person to help him
make it big. But Jake can't shake the creepy feeling he gets when
he visits Augustus's performance space. Can it be true that The
Marvelous Melbourne haunts the theater? And did he really die
inside the Spirit Cabinet--the box Jake ends up trapped inside
during Towers' stage premiere? For whatever reason, Jake can't
breathe in there. . . .

ISBN: 978-1-4965-7911-9 (library hardcover)
ISBN: 978-1-4965-7913-3 (ebook PDF)

Printed and bound in the USA.
PA48

MICHAEL DAHL PRESENTS

Michael Dahl has written about werewolves, magicians, and superheroes. He loves funny books, scary books, and mysterious books. Every Michael Dahl Presents book is chosen by Michael himself and written by an author he loves. The books are about favorite subjects like monster aliens, haunted houses, farting pigs, or magical powers that go haywire. Read on!

CLAUSTROPHOBIA
(klaw-struh-FOH-bee-uh)

THE FEAR OF
SMALL SPACES

EVERYONE IS AFRAID OF SOMETHING.

I'm afraid of quite a number of things. But a PHOBIA is a very special fear. It is deep and strong and long lasting. It is hard to explain why people have phobias—they just do.

Ever since the age of five, when my cousins locked me in a big toy chest, I've been terrified of small spaces. Just like Jake in this story. I don't know how he can prowl around that spooky basement or step inside the Spirit Cabinet. It reminds me too much of that old chest!

Michael Dahl

1

The Biggest Little City in the World. That's what the neon sign outside town said. People came to Reno, Nevada, to test their luck. They wanted to turn one dollar into a whole stack. They wanted to make their dreams come true. They wanted to see something . . . *magical.*

The brilliant lights that gave Reno its glow were on 24/7, but they didn't really shine until the sun dipped behind the Sierra Nevada mountains. Then the town really came alive. Performers brought buckets and blankets and stood on the sidewalks. They put on displays—juggling, dancing, standing very still (I swear, there's a guy named Vinnie who does it)—and people strolled around, watching. When the show was over, they dropped money into the buckets and went on their way.

I was one of those performers.

It was a hot spring afternoon, and I had my table set up on the sidewalk. A small crowd of people were gathered around me. They were all tourists. They were *always* tourists. On top of the table I had three red cups and a bright orange Ping-Pong ball. It was an old trick known as—big shocker—"cup and ball."

"OK, everyone," I said, bouncing the ball on the table. "The game is simple. Keep your eye on the ball. I'm going to slide it under one of the cups, shuffle the cups around, and you're going to tell me where it is. Got it?"

The crowd nodded and mumbled. One woman in front, an older lady, clutched her purse to her chest.

I lifted my Golden Knights cap off my head. "There's nothing under my hat," I said, making a show of it. I replaced the cap and pulled up both sleeves of my jacket. "And nothing up my sleeves. Are you ready?"

They cried, "Yes!" in unison.

I lifted the cup in the middle and slipped the ball under. "Here we go."

I quickly slid the cups around on the table, weaving them in and out and around, trying to be unpredictable.

Finally, I stopped. "Now, place your bets. Set your money on the table near the cup you think the ball is under."

A few people came forward and dropped one-dollar and five-dollar bills next to the cup on the right. The lady with the purse was a big spender. She set a folded ten-dollar bill beside it.

With my left hand, I lifted the cup they'd chosen. Underneath, it was empty. "Oh, so sorry," I said. I grabbed the middle cup with my right hand and picked it up. The orange ball sat there.

I scooped up the money. "Who wants to try again?"

Any magician will tell you that magic is mostly just trickery. There's nothing supernatural about it at all. It's all misdirection and practice. Lots of practice.

So here's the thing. I *never* put the ball under the middle cup at all. I only made it look like I did. The ball never left my hand. Not until the end of the trick, when I dropped it under the middle cup—the cup no one had chosen.

The group of tourists shuffled away, grumbling about the money they'd just lost to a kid. Then I started the trick over with a new wave of tourists. I pretended to slip the ball under the middle cup, shuffled them around. Shouted, "Place your bets!" as they stacked money on the table.

Only this time, a voice in the back said, "Show us your right hand."

My right hand. Where the orange ball was hidden in my palm.

The man who'd made the request stood in the back of the group. He was tall, with slicked-back black hair. He had deep creases in his face, and a wide smile. He looked like a cop.

The police officer would show everyone I was still holding the orange ball. Then he'd ask for my performing license. But he already knew I was too young to have one.

The jig was up.

Panicked, I flipped the table over, sending money and cups flying. I turned and darted down the sidewalk, running into the first alley I could find.

As I dashed between the brick walls, they seemed to close in on me. My chest tightened. Ahead, the alley ended with a cement wall too high to climb over. It was a dead-end.

I skidded to a stop. I could feel the man's presence behind me.

"Listen," I said as I turned. It was hard to breathe. I felt like a rat trapped in a maze. "I have a license, I swear. It's just . . . I don't have it on me."

The man had his hands in his pockets. Maybe he wasn't a cop after all. Maybe he was just a rube whose money I stole, and he was looking to get it back. I pulled the wad of bills out of my pocket. "Just take it all," I said.

The man laughed. "Put it away, kid," he said. "I'm not here to bust you. I'm here to help you."

2

"Help me?" Words barely snuck past my lips. I needed to get away, get out. The narrow alleyway almost seemed like it was caving in on me. But I was curious about the man in front of me.

"Your sleight-of-hand work was impressive," the man said. "The skill and quickness in your hands to hide that ball was really well done. What's your name?"

I hesitated a moment, then said, "Jake. Jake Prescott."

With a flourish, the man withdrew a hand from his pocket. Between two fingers was a business card. He held it out to me. "Pleasure to meet you, Jake. The name's Augustus Towers."

Augustus Towers? I thought. *Why does that sound familiar?*

The card was vibrant red with black, glittering cursive. *Augustus Towers, Illusionist.*

"You're that magician," I said. It was supposed to be a question, but it didn't come out that way.

"Indeed," Towers said. "And I'm about to make my mark in this town. Care to be a part of that?"

"How?" I asked.

"My assistant and I could use an extra pair of hands." Towers bowed. "There's an address on the back of the card," he said. "If you decide to take me up on the offer, that's where you'll find me. You have skills, Jake Prescott. And I can help you polish them."

With that, Towers walked away and disappeared out of the alley. I was finally free. I dashed out of that narrow, creepy alley, back out into the street. I put my hands on my knees, trying to catch my breath. I glanced left, then right.

Towers was gone.

My table was upturned but still there, the cups resting in the gutter. I gathered my things, folded up the table, and carried it home tucked under one arm.

My parents and I lived in an apartment building in a section of Reno that my dad calls "vintage." Vintage meant old. Old meant run-down. We lived on the fifth floor. Instead of using the ancient elevator, I always took the stairs. Elevators freak me out. Small spaces freak me out.

"Hello?" I called out when I walked into our apartment. I didn't expect an answer. My dad was always at the Lucky Draw, where he dealt cards all hours of the day. My mom was across the street from him at Slotsville!, serving food and beverages at the restaurant with the "best buffet in Reno" (according to its owner).

I hated our apartment, hated my room even more. It was small, cramped. If I stood on my tiptoes, my fingertips could graze the ceiling. The first thing I did when I entered my bedroom was

shove open my window. At least then I could close my eyes, hear the noise from the sidewalks, and pretend I wasn't stuck in a tiny room.

My thin bedroom walls were covered with old posters of magicians. Harry Houdini. Carter the Great. Mr. Madagascar. Clothes covered my floor, and a stack of books on card tricks and illusions sat on my nightstand. I ditched the card table in my closet, stuck the wad of cash in my sock drawer, and fell face-first onto the bed.

You have skills, Towers had said. *I can help you polish them.*

What did that mean?

I pulled the business card out of my pocket, flipped it over, and looked at the address on the back. *1101 Desert Drive*. Not far away. About a block off 395, down near the Truckee River.

I sat alone in the dark, listening to the car horns, the hoots and hollers, the world outside my window. I loved magic, everything about it. And if Augustus Towers wanted to help me work toward becoming a magician, then I was definitely going to take him up on his offer.

3

It was a boarded-up theater. Broken marquee. Half the globe light bulbs shattered, the other half burnt out. A darkened neon sign—whose cursive letters matched the font on Towers's business card—called it the *Regal Theatre*. It was anything but regal.

I'd waited until after school to walk to 1101 Desert Drive. I wasn't expecting a closed theater with giant plywood panels covered in flyers and graffiti blocking the doors and windows.

This was a mistake, I thought.

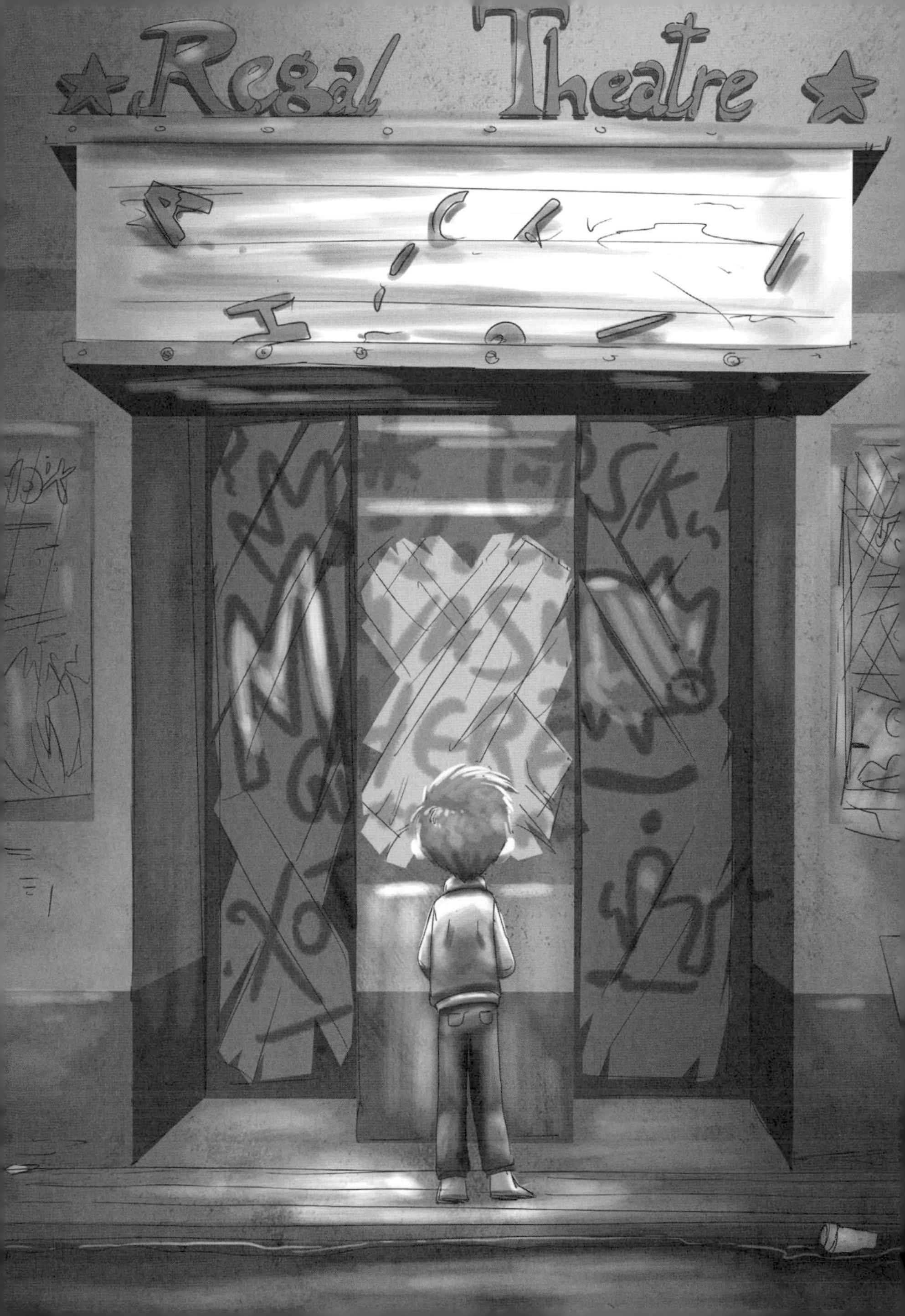
Regal Theatre

Towers was either crazy or a scam artist. I cursed myself for ever getting up the hope that he would help a kid like me.

"Hey! You came!"

While I was feeling sorry for myself, Augustus Towers had exited one of the theater's side doors and come around the front. He was walking toward me, arms extended like I was an old friend.

"Um . . . hi," was all I could say.

"What do you think of the place?" Towers gestured toward the theater with one arm with the kind of flourish only a magician had.

"It . . . needs some work," I replied.

Towers laughed. "Yes, it certainly does. But I have grand designs. Come. Let me show you around."

Towers led me to a side door that had once been boarded closed. The two-by-fours that had been pried off were still leaning against the brick wall beside it.

Inside, the boarded-up doors and windows made the theater dark and musty. Years of dust and grime covered every inch of the spacious lobby, from the ticket counter to the spiral staircase to the glass chandelier hanging high above us. I caught myself holding my breath, afraid to breathe in the swirling, angry dust clouds we created with each step.

"It will take hard work to get it shiny and new again," Towers said. "But it will be worth it."

Wait. Am I just here to do manual labor?

"Are you familiar with a magician named The Marvelous Melbourne?" Towers asked.

I nodded.

"Of course you are." Towers smiled. "I like you, Jake Prescott. Anyway, Melbourne used to perform exclusively at the Regal. Well, that is, until . . ." Towers trailed off, but he didn't need to finish the sentence. The Marvelous Melbourne's real claim to fame as a magician had to do with his death.

"I found the key to the backstage door," came a voice behind me.

A woman in her twenties stood behind me, one hand on her hip, the other holding out a ring of old keys. She was beautiful, with shoulder-length hair so blond it was almost white. She looked confident and strong, and I immediately shrank back with nervousness.

"Thank you, Luna," Towers said. He nodded at me. "Luna, dear, this is Jake Prescott. Jake, this is my assistant, Luna Kellar."

"Charmed," Luna said. She looked me over, not sounding charmed at all.

Luna spun on a heel and walked out of the lobby. She led us down a narrow hallway. I could feel my breath starting to rasp, feel my heartbeat race. I did my best to hold it together as we reached a door at the end of the hall.

Using one of the keys—long and ancient-looking, like a skeleton key from an old pirate movie—Luna unlocked the door. Behind it a set of stairs led down into a sea of blackness. Without hesitation, Luna stepped into the dark.

"After you," Towers said to me, nodding at the doorway.

Trying not to panic, I began to descend the creaky stairs.

4

I was halfway down the steps when the blackness was washed away by light.

"Finally," Luna said from the bottom. "A spot where the electricity actually works."

"Oh, thank you," I whispered to fate or to a higher power or to The Marvelous Melbourne.

The bare bulbs dangling from the beams above were blazing. They didn't totally cure my fear of tight spaces, but they did help a little. The basement was dust overload. Cobwebs were everywhere, so weighed down by dust that they drooped and split. The pockets of light created harsh shadows on the walls.

"It's larger than I thought," Towers marveled. The basement stretched further than I could see, its ceiling higher than the one in my apartment.

"We're directly under the stage, Augustus," Luna explained. She pointed to the middle of the room. "There's where the trap door comes down."

"This way. Quickly." Towers had spotted something. Like a curious child he scurried toward it.

Wooden crates and pallets of boxes lined one wall. Towers examined them.

"Jackpot," he said. "They're all stamped with The Marvelous Melbourne's initials."

"His illusions?" Luna's interest was sparked by the discovery of the tools and devices Melbourne used on stage in his magic shows.

"Every one of them," Towers said. He and Luna hugged. "This is what we've been searching for."

"Oh, Augustus!"

Towers released Luna and waved me over. "Jake," he said. "Come here."

I hesitantly walked over. Luna began investigating

a crate with a number stenciled on its side. Towers slid a box from the stack and peeled open the top. It was filled with books and metal contraptions I didn't recognize.

"His journals, his illusions . . . everything!" Towers said. "All left by his estate after his death. This is wonderful!" He picked up a journal and began to flip through it.

I thought it was pretty cool, but my attention had turned to the larger contraptions beyond the crates. One of them was a glass tank, like the kind Harry Houdini would suspend himself in upside down and fill with water. Another looked like a guillotine used to lop off heads. And there was a box that looked like Carter the Great's "Elongated Woman" illusion.

But the one that had my attention, like a magnet was drawing me toward it, was a blood-red cabinet with wispy white ghosts painted on the side. There were two door panels on the front.

"What is this illusion?"

My words were swallowed by the basement, and neither Towers nor Luna heard.

I walked toward the cabinet, like I was pulled by an invisible string. I placed the palm of my hand on its side, near one of the ghosts. The shadows draped over the illusion seemed almost to part as I touched it. The whispers grew louder. *Look inside,* they seemed to say.

I opened one of the door panels, peering into the box. It wasn't very large—just the size for a willing assistant to squeeze through. I'd seen plenty of illusions like it. Cabinets where magicians made assistants shrink and grow, where they sawed them in half, where they stuck swords inside to the delighted gasps of the crowd.

But I'd never seen an illusion like this.

The painted ghosts were not just on the outside. They seemed to cover the cabinet's interior as well. I stepped inside for a closer look, digging in my pocket for my phone so I could use the flashlight app to see better.

SLAM!

The door to the illusion banged shut behind me.

5

My breath caught in my throat. "Help!" I choked out as I banged my open palms on the wooden cabinet door.

"Jake!" I heard Towers rush over. He rattled the door handles. "Jake! Remain calm!"

I could feel the sweat pour down my face. My hands trembled and stung.

And then Towers pried the door open.

I fell forward onto the cold cement floor. Towers knelt next to me. Luna stood behind him.

"Are you OK?" Towers asked.

"Cabinet just . . . closed," I croaked out. "Trapped . . ."

"You're OK now," Towers said. He helped me to my feet. "Come on, let's get you upstairs and into the fresh air. Luna and I will explore this later."

By the time we were back in the lobby, I was starting to feel calm again. When we stepped into the sunny afternoon heat, it was like the incident had never happened.

"I hope this hasn't turned you away from being our new assistant," Towers joked.

"No, sir," I said. "I'll be back tomorrow."

"Good."

While he smiled, I caught Luna's sour expression at his use of the word "assistant."

I couldn't sleep.

I laid in bed, staring up at the ceiling. The breeze from the open window slid across me while the sounds of Reno nightlife filled the room.

The feeling of being trapped in the cabinet was

still strong. But more than that, I couldn't stop thinking about The Marvelous Melbourne.

I hadn't lied to Towers. I knew Melbourne's name. But I didn't know the details of his death. So I sat up in bed and grabbed my laptop from the floor.

One quick browser search, and I had Melbourne's biography. There was a trick deck of cards on my nightstand. To keep my nervous hands busy, I began to riffle through them, practicing my cuts and forces as I read.

The bio for Jonathan Melbourne talked about his poverty-stricken childhood in New Orleans. His marriage to Betty Farmer, one of his assistants. His career as an illusionist in California, then Nevada.

But the section I was most curious about was the one labeled "Death."

"The death of Jonathan Melbourne is shrouded in mystery," I read aloud. Riffle, cut. Shuffle, cut. "At the age of 43, Melbourne was at the height of his popularity. Sell-out crowds filled the Regal Theatre in Reno, Nevada, each night. On August 3, 1948, while performing an illusion known as the Spirit Cabinet, Melbourne failed to emerge within the allotted time. Stagehands forced the cabinet open, finding Melbourne dead inside. His death was listed as natural causes, but the truth is not fully understood."

I stopped reading. Stopped shuffling. Goose bumps spread like tidal waves down my arms as I saw the illustrated poster displayed below the biography. *The Marvelous Melbourne and his Spirit Cabinet!* Beneath the words, surrounded by swirling ghosts, was The Marvelous Melbourne.

Beside him was the giant cabinet I'd been locked in that afternoon.

As if that wasn't enough, the last line of the article said, "The ghost of The Marvelous Melbourne is said to haunt the Regal Theatre. After a series of strange occurrences (whispering voices, phantom lights, etc.), its doors were shuttered for good in 1983."

I slammed the laptop shut, its light winking out and leaving me in the dark once again.

6

I'm standing in the spotlight, on stage at the Regal
Theatre with The Marvelous Melbourne. Melbourne
waves his magic wand, and from the shadows,
the Spirit Cabinet appears. But as it draws near, the
cabinet shifts and moves. Ghosts float around it.
The cabinet changes shape until—

—it's a coffin.

"Ladies and gentlemen, let's give him a hand!"
Melbourne boasts as he shoves me into the coffin and
slams the lid closed.

"Help!" I scream as—

I woke up covered in sweat. My legs were tangled in my sheets. I kicked and clawed them away, climbing out of bed and walking to the open window. It was almost dawn, an orange haze on the horizon. The city, never fully asleep, still rustled and thrummed.

I rested my arms on the windowsill and leaned my head out. Closed my eyes. Tried to forget the nightmare.

I never fell back to sleep.

I don't know why I decided to go back to the Regal Theatre after school. Maybe I just wanted to tell Towers what I'd learned about The Marvelous Melbourne, to see if he knew the story. Maybe I just wanted another look at the Spirit Cabinet.

When I got to the Regal, I knocked loudly on the side door we'd used the day before. The front doors were still boarded up. No one answered. I tried again and got the same response. After waiting a minute, I tried the door handle and found it unlocked.

"Hello?" I called out once I'd reached the lobby.

Cu-clunk.

The sound came from beyond the swinging lobby doors. I walked through them to find rows of empty, broken red-velvet chairs that led down to a lighted stage. On the stage was what looked like a giant milk can, the kind Harry Houdini used in his escapes. It was metal, about three feet high, and shaped kind of like a vase.

The milk can moved. *Cu-clunk.*

I jumped back. *Did that really just happen?* Thoughts of The Marvelous Melbourne's ghost clouded my mind.

I crept up the aisle toward the stage. Even though several spotlights shone down on the milk can, it seemed as if it were cloaked in shadow. I climbed the stage steps, and the shadows receded.

I reached out. My fingers grazed the top of the milk can's cool metal surface.

Cu-CLUNK.

"Ah!" I stumbled back and fell.

The lid of the milk can swung open and Luna emerged.

"What are you doing?" she asked, unfolding her body from the cramped space and standing.

"I . . . I just . . ."

"Augustus isn't here," she said abruptly.

The thought of a haunted theater was still rattling around in my head.

"Is that . . . ?" I pointed at the milk can.

"From downstairs?" Luna nodded. "Brought it up this morning." She brushed past me, bumping my shoulder as she went. "I can do this escape in my sleep," she continued. "But this can is rusted and old. Took a little extra to get free. Want to try?"

She motioned to the milk can, a smile creeping over her face. She knew how I reacted the last time I'd been stuck in an illusion. Did she want me to fail?

"No thanks," I said. There was something about the can, the way the shadows crept over it, that gave me a bad feeling.

"Oh, come on," Luna urged me. She stepped closer. "If you wanna be Augustus's assistant, you can't be afraid of a little old magic trick."

"Jake!" Towers strolled down the aisle, a brown paper bag cradled in one arm. "You've decided to return!"

Towers took the steps to the stage two at a time. Luna hadn't moved. Her eyes pierced daggers at me. Towers didn't notice, though. He plopped the bag into her arms. "Here you are, Luna," he said. He brushed off his hands. As he did, a deck of cards appeared in them.

"Voilà!" He did a waterfall flourish with the cards. They danced from one hand to the other. "Come! Let me show you a few simple card tricks."

Towers walked toward a table in the stage wing. I glanced over my shoulder. The shadows that had surrounded the milk can had spread. Now they appeared to stretch toward Luna's legs and feet.

She hadn't moved. Her eyes followed us. Her sneer seen only by me.

7

Days passed.

And the nightmares kept coming.

In all of them, The Marvelous Melbourne forced me into illusions—milk cans, water tanks, the Spirit Cabinet—as I gasped for breath.

I walked around with bags under my eyes, and used my lack of sleep to justify the weird things I saw every time I visited the Regal. Shadows lingered on the milk can—on everything. And it wasn't just shadows.

There were times when I stood onstage, and the temperature plummeted until I could see my breath in front of my face. But only for a moment. And then it was gone.

I tried to explain it to Towers, but he just claimed the theater was old, and the air conditioning must have been on the fritz. When I described the shadows to Luna, she just rolled her eyes and ignored me.

Slowly, we cleaned the theater. Just the three of us. It required special masks and goggles, so we wouldn't breathe in dust and cobwebs. Towers pried the plywood from the lobby's front doors, paid to replace the glass, and left the doors wide open as we worked.

One afternoon, a cherry-picker truck arrived. Two men raised it up, slowly testing and replacing the bulbs in the marquee that hung out over the sidewalk. Luna and I watched them work.

Days of hard work were followed by nights of magic. Towers and I would spend hours on stage at the Regal, doing everything from card tricks to small illusions. Once he even tried to wheel the Spirit Cabinet out onto the stage. He slipped a rolled-up journal from his back pocket and slapped it against his other palm.

"Come, Jake!" he said. "With Melbourne's journal, we can master the Spirit Cabinet!"

Just the sight of the cabinet made my stomach turn. "No thanks," I said.

"Don't let the stories about Melbourne frighten you," Towers said. "Ghosts are mere fabrication. Made up!"

But it wasn't just the stories that terrified me. It was the nightmares and shadows. Even at that moment, the shadows appeared to shift and grow around the cabinet.

"I'm . . . I'm not feeling so well," I said, turning to exit and hide out in the restroom. Luna was in the aisle, watching us with her arms folded across her chest.

One night soon after, I reached my breaking point.

When I reached the theater, the marquee lights flickered and faltered in the evening light. That should have been my cue to turn around and go right back home.

Instead, I tried the front door. It was unlocked.

"Hello?" I called into the pristine lobby. No reply.

"Hello? Augustus? Luna?" I called out to an empty stage. No reply.

They must be in the basement, I thought.

I hadn't been in the basement since that fateful first day. I made my way down the narrow hallway. Sure enough, the door to the basement was open, light shining from below.

"Hello?" I called again.

This time, Towers shouted back. "Down here, Jake!"

I tried to control my breathing as I descended the narrow stairs.

The basement was awash in pockets of light. I could see Towers and Luna on the far side of the basement, near the stacks of boxes. I started to walk over, dropping out of one pool of light and into the shadows, then back into the light.

As I passed by the looming water tank, I suddenly slipped and fell hard onto the cement floor. My right elbow cracked hard, and pain shot down to my fingers.

"Oof!"

"Jake!"

By the time Towers reached me, I was up on my knees, massaging my injured arm.

"What happened?" Towers asked.

"I slipped on . . ." I looked beside me, where a puddle of water sat in the cement. It was out of place, glinting in the harsh light. It had the outline of a shoe. And beside it was another pool of water. A third. A fourth. One after the other, all shaped like footsteps. And they were leading away from . . .

"The water tank," I whispered.

"What?" Towers was confused.

"Look!" I pointed at the puddles. "They're footsteps. Of someone walking away from the tank."

"Nonsense!" Towers scoffed. He walked over to the tank and ran a finger along the glass. It left a

smudge. "We haven't touched the tank yet. It's dry as can be! There must be a leaky pipe. I'll track it down when I have a spare moment." He tilted his head to eyeball the ceiling, looking for a water pipe.

But my gut told me it wasn't a leaky pipe. *Because it's a ghost!* I nearly shouted. It was a ridiculous explanation, but I couldn't shake it. The ghost of The Marvelous Melbourne was fooling with us. And as I looked at the tank, the shadows around it began to grow again. Whispers floated and bubbled through the air. The shadows took shape behind the tank. And the shape looked just like a person.

"That's it," I muttered. I stepped away from the tank. "I'm . . . sorry."

"It's OK, Jake," Towers said.

"No . . . I'm sorry." My chest began to squeeze, like my ribs were the teeth of a steel trap. "I can't do this, Mr. Towers. I can't help you out anymore."

And as fast as my legs would carry me, I ran for the steps, for the lobby.

Even with Augustus Towers shouting after me in protest, I ran to escape.

8

"OK, everyone," I said, bouncing the Ping-Pong ball on the table. "The game is simple. Keep your eye on the orange ball. I'm going to slide it under one of the cups, shuffle the cups around, and you're going to tell me where it is. Got it?"

I was back on the street. Back at my table. A crowd was gathered around me, ready to lose their money.

It had been a month since my last visit to Regal Theatre. The nightmares about The Marvelous Melbourne were a memory, like a fever that had broken.

"OK," I said, lifting the first cup. "And away we—"

A bus rumbled by on the street, distracting me. Plastered on its side was the smiling face of Augustus Towers.

OPENING NIGHT! the sign read. *SEE TOWERS TAME THE TREACHEROUS TANK ESCAPE!*

"Excuse me?" A man in front fanned me with his cash, breaking my stare. "Are you gonna do the trick or what?"

I returned to my trick, letting the group win the first round (to lure them in) before taking their money the next three times.

I thought about Augustus the whole walk home. When I reached the apartment and had stowed my table, I pulled from under my bed a flyer I'd been handed outside the Lucky Draw one afternoon. It was the same image of Augustus, only this one had an additional image of him inside the water tank.

I could almost hear the whispers, see the shadows.

It was too much to pass up.

My parents, as usual, were at work. I didn't leave a note, just threw on my coat and headed back out to walk the familiar route to the Regal Theatre.

The marquee was brighter than ever. The name *Regal* burned red in the dusky evening glow. It probably hadn't looked that way since The Marvelous Melbourne had performed there.

A crowd lingered outside, snapping photos and chatting. I was suddenly worried that the show would be sold out.

"One, please," I said to the old woman in the ticket window. "I don't care which section."

She eyed me up. Her glasses made her eyes look comically huge. "Your name wouldn't be Jake Prescott, would it?"

I was taken aback. "Uh . . . yeah, actually," I answered.

The woman pulled an envelope from the register and slid it across to me. "He thought you might show up." The envelope had my name written on it, along with the word *FREE*.

The renovation of the Regal Theatre was complete, and it was stunning. A glittering crystal chandelier had replaced the dusty old one in the lobby. The concession area had all-new glass and a vintage popcorn machine.

The lights above flickered and dimmed. My heart fluttered in my chest until I realized it was intentional, as the crowds began to filter into the theater.

The show was about to begin.

I found my seat near the front, right near the aisle.

Before long, the lights in the theater dimmed. Spotlights illuminated the stage. The red curtain peeled back, and Augustus Towers emerged to applause. He wore a suit coat with tails and a top hat. He looked just like the photo I'd seen of The Marvelous Melbourne.

"Ladies and gentlemen, boys and girls!" Towers's voice boomed. "Prepare yourself to step back in time! When the Regal was regal and The Marvelous Melbourne wowed young and old alike!"

The crowd roared its approval as the curtains parted all the way and Luna appeared alongside the first illusion: the Sawed Lady.

For the next hour, Towers held the audience captive with his illusions. He performed card tricks that mystified. He made Luna disappear in one tall, narrow box and appear in another box on the opposite side of the stage. He produced dove after dove from his top hat. The crowd ate it up.

Finally, the lights winked out, leaving the theater in darkness. The crowd murmured. A spotlight directly over the stage suddenly lit up. Beneath it was Melbourne's water tank. It was no longer empty and coated in dust. Instead it was filled with sloshing water.

The hair on the back of my neck rose. Towers and Luna emerged from the dark. "And now," Towers began. "I shall attempt my greatest feat yet. The Treacherous Tank Escape! Handcuffed and locked into the tank, I will somehow manage to emerge from certain death!"

The crowd went quiet as Luna brought out a pair

of handcuffs. She held them high, showing them off to the audience. Then, as orchestral music played, she locked Towers's hands together. He climbed a set of stairs behind the tank and dropped in with a small splash, suit coat, top hat, and all.

The crowd gasped. Luna slid the heavy metal lid of the tank over the top. It clanged ominously into place. A pair of padlocks hung on either side, and she snapped them both shut, wiggling them to let the audience know they were truly locked. Then she brought out a large red tapestry and draped it over the tank, hiding the submerged Towers from sight.

I crept up in my seat until I was on the edge. The shadows were back, sliding across the tapestry, wrapping themselves around the tank. Was I the only one who saw them?

Seconds ticked by. Then a whole minute. *Where is he?* I wondered. *Is this just for effect? Or is something wrong?*

It had to be effect. He was making the illusion look harder than it was. Right? *Right?*

When the third minute clicked by and Towers had not yet surfaced, a pit grew in my stomach.

"Something's wrong," I whispered. Soon whispers seemed to roll like waves through the crowd until they reached the stage.

"It's OK!" Luna shouted in an attempt to calm the masses. "Everything is all right! I'll show you!"

She reached for the tapestry and began to pull. It didn't budge. The shadows seemed to hold it in place. Luna yanked with all her might.

Finally the tapestry came free, knocking her to the stage floor.

The crowd gasped. Augustus Towers was still in the tank. Still handcuffed.

And completely still.

9

"He's drowned!" a woman near the front screamed.

I was on my feet, running toward the stage as the stunned, confused crowd tried to figure out what was happening. That was the thing with magic. It was hard to sort out truth from illusion.

But I knew that Towers was in real danger.

I leapt up on stage as Luna hurried to the wings. She returned seconds later, an ax in her hand.

I slammed my fists against the glass. "Augustus!" I shouted.

His eyes suddenly flew open. Bubbles gurgled from his mouth.

"He's still alive!" I cried out.

Behind us, the crowd was in a frenzy. Some rushed for the exits to get help. Others had their phones out, recording the tragic event. Many stood rooted in place, shocked at what they were witnessing.

Luna reared back and swung the ax. It struck the tank's thick glass. A crack appeared in the glass. I stumbled back, watching the crack grow bigger. The shadows moved in, as if trying to hold the tank together. Luna wound up for another swing.

She didn't need it. The tank shattered forcefully. Water gushed out like a tidal wave. It soaked me, Luna, the stage. The audience members who were still in the theater screamed and retreated to safety.

Towers lay limp in the now-empty tank. I staggered to my feet and ran over to him. He'd fainted again. But I could see his chest rising and falling.

Rising and falling.

Paramedics arrived shortly after. They carefully lifted the semi-conscious Towers out of the tank, past the jagged shards of glass left over from Luna's major-league swing. They loaded him onto a gurney and wheeled him up the aisle. "Will he be OK?" Luna asked one of the EMTs.

The EMT shrugged. "We're hopeful," he said. "But it's uncertain right now."

And then they were gone. The stage was silent, the night ruined. Social media posts were probably already spreading like fire across the internet. There was no coming back from this. The Regal revival was finished.

Towers' act was "one night only."

Luna and I were the only ones remaining. I studied the shell of the water tank. Broken glass like teeth on one side. The other side still holding the lid in place at the top. Thin streaks of water still coursed down it. They soaked into the wooden stage.

Luna wrung out Towers's sodden suit coat, left by the EMTs.

"I know what happened tonight," I stated matter-of-factly.

This, more than anything I'd said before, got Luna's attention.

"The spirit of The Marvelous Melbourne," I stated. "It's haunting the theater. I . . . I can see shadows all around. They made it hard for you to pull the tapestry off the tank."

The set of trick handcuffs used in the illusion—easy to pop open with the right key, which Towers would have kept tucked under his tongue or his inside cheek—lay on the wet stage. I scooped them up. "The ghost even made it hard for him to take off—"

I stopped and felt the weight of the handcuffs in my palm. They weren't trick handcuffs at all. Someone had switched them out. Someone had wanted Towers to fail.

I turned back to Luna. A devilish grin slowly crept across her face.

"Oops," she said. "Busted."

10

"It was *you*?" I whispered. The handcuffs slipped from my fingers and clattered on the wooden stage floor. "But how? I heard the whispers. I saw the shadows. The ghost of The Marvelous Melbourne haunts the theater, and he was trying to kill Augustus."

Luna threw her head back and laughed. "Ghost! Ha! You child. There's no such thing as ghosts. Just envious assistants who no longer want to live in the shadows of their inferior boss."

Luna stepped toward me. I stumbled back, out of the spotlight.

"Towers is a joke now," Luna continued. "This theater will be shut down, boarded up again."

As Luna spoke, I backed toward the darkened wings of the stage.

Behind her, the shadows around the water tank began to move. They were forming into a shape. The silhouette of a human.

The ghost of The Marvelous Melbourne.

I held out one arm, pointed with one shaking finger. "Luna," I croaked.

Luna turned, and the shadows pounced.
I stumbled backward toward the wings, scared and trying hard to escape. I tripped and fell and my back slammed into something hard. I looked around and saw painted ghosts floating to my left, my right, above.

I had fallen into the open Spirit Cabinet!

Just as I made this terrifying realization, the cabinet's doors slammed shut.

"Noooooo!"

I shoved my body against the doors. But they didn't budge. I could feel my heart race, my breath coming in ragged, shallow gulps. My mouth and tongue felt like I'd swallowed sand.

A blood-curdling scream echoed through the theater. There was a thin gap between the cabinet doors, a sliver of spotlight. I squinted, tried to look out, and saw Luna wrestling with shadows.

And then, with a final, stifled scream, she disappeared into them, like she had been swallowed whole.

All that remained on the stage was the outline of a man made of shadow. Top hat. Tails. The ghost of The Marvelous Melbourne.

"Help!" I bellowed. It was no use. There was nobody inside the theater anymore.

I was trapped.

The walls of the Spirit Cabinet closed in on me. The whispers washed over me. They seemed to be coming from the painted ghosts. I was starting to hyperventilate. I took quick breaths, wiping sweat from my brow with one palm. I was suffocating and was helpless to stop it.

Through the sliver in the doors, I saw The Marvelous Melbourne take center stage. Shadows swarmed around him. The ghost took off his top hat, held it to his chest with one hand, and took a long, graceful bow.

The spotlight winked off.

GLOSSARY

allotted (uh-LAHT-id)—set aside for a particular purpose

fabrication (fab-rik-AY-shuhn)—something made up in order to trick someone

guillotine (GIL-uh-teen)—machine for executing people by beheading them

hyperventilate (hye-pur-VENT-uh-layt)—to breathe rapidly

inferior (in-FIHR-ee-ur)—of low standard or quality

marquee (mar-KEE)—a structure over the entrance to a theater that tells audiences what will be showing or playing

misdirection (mis-duh-REK-shuhn)—the act of directing someone to the wrong place

paramedic (PAR-uh-MED-ik)—a person who is trained to give emergency medical treatment but who is not a doctor or a nurse

recede (ri-SEED)—to move back

renovation (ren-uh-VAY-shuhn)—the action of fixing up a building

silhouette (SIH-loo-ett)—an outline of a person or object filled in with a solid dark color

stagehand (STAYJ-hand)—a person who moves scenery or props during a performance

submerge (suhb-MURJ)—to push below the surface of the water

tapestry (TAP-i-stree)—a heavy piece of cloth

trickery (TRIK-er-ee)—the practice of tricking someone

upturn (uhp-TURN)—to flip something over or make disorderly

vintage (VIN-tij)—from the past

FACE YOUR FEAR!

Now that you've read the story, it's no longer only inside this book. It's also in your brain. Can your brain help you answer the prompts below?

1. Jake has trouble sleeping, and starts seeing weirder things in the theater when he's tired. Write about a time you thought you saw something in the dark when you were tired.

2. Luna acts jealous of Jake for being Towers's assistant. Discuss how you would have felt if you had to work with her.

3. Why do you think Jake is drawn to the glass tank illusion before he knows the history behind it?

4. Would you make the same choices as Jake if you were in his place? Write a short story about what you would do if you had to work with Towers.

5. Write what you think happens next in the story after the last chapter. Does Jake escape, or is he doomed?

FEAR FACTORS

claustrophobia (klaw-struh-FOH-bee-uh)—the fear of small spaces

Jake's phobia is one I share with him. (Remember that toy chest?) Some experts believe that five percent of the world's population is affected by claustrophobia. That's more than three hundred million people! So if you have this fear, you're not alone.

In the 1800s, many people in the United States had a specific type of claustrophobia: taphephobia (taf-uh-FOH-bee-uh), the fear of being buried alive. So safety coffins were made with bells or other alarms that a person could use signaling for help—just in case they woke up and found themselves six feet under by mistake.

Edgar Allan Poe, the great master of horror literature, often wrote short stories where people were buried alive or trapped in small spaces. His best-known ones are "The Cask of Amontillado," "The Fall of the House of Usher," and "The Premature Burial." Premature means "happening too soon"!

Claustrophobics (people with claustrophobia) are not simply afraid of crowded, closed-in places. They're nervous around places that are hard to get out of, like elevators, basements, tunnels, or rooms without windows. Even sitting in a dentist's chair can trigger this phobia!

ABOUT THE AUTHOR

Brandon Terrell has been a lifelong fan of all things spooky, scary, and downright creepy. He is the author of numerous children's books including several volumes in Capstone's Spine Shivers and Snoops, Inc. series. When not hunched over his laptop writing, Brandon enjoys watching movies (horror movies, especially!), reading, baseball, and spending time with his wife and two children in Minnesota.

ABOUT THE ILLUSTRATOR

Mariano Epelbaum is a character designer, illustrator, and

traditional 2D animator. He has been working as a professional artist since 1996, and enjoys trying different art styles and techniques. Throughout his career Mariano has created characters and designs for a wide range of films, TV series, commercials, and publications in his native country of Argentina. In addition to Michael Dahl Presents: Phobia, Mariano has also contributed to the Fairy Tale Mix-ups, You Choose: Fractured Fairy Tales, and Snoops, Inc. series for Capstone.